GAZELLE

NEVER KISS FROGS!

by

ROBERT LEESON

Illustrated by David Simonds

HAMISH HAMILTON
LONDON

HAMISH HAMILTON LTD

Published by the Penguin Group
Penguin Books Ltd, 27 Wrights Lane, London, W8 5TZ, England
Penguin Books USA Inc., 375 Hudson Street, New York, New York 10014, USA
Penguin Books Australia Ltd, Ringwood, Victoria, Australia
Penguin Books Canada Ltd, 10 Alcorn Avenue, Toronto, Ontario, Canada M4V 3B.
Penguin Books (NZ) Ltd, 182-190 Wairau Road, Auckland 10, New Zealand

Penguin Books Ltd, Registered Offices: Harmondsworth, Middlesex, England

First published in Great Britain 1988 by Hamish Hamilton Ltd

Copyright © 1988 by Robert Leeson
Illustrations copyright © 1988 by David Simonds

The moral rights of the author and artist have been asserted

5 7 9 10 8 6 4

Set in 15pt Baskerville by Rowland Phototypesetting Ltd
Bury St Edmunds, Suffolk
Printed in Great Britain by BPCC Hazell Books Ltd,
Member of BPCC Ltd, Aylesbury, Bucks

A CIP catalogue record for this book is available from the British Library

ISBN 0–241–12489–1

Chapter One

Gail was a nice girl. Sometimes she behaved well. Sometimes she behaved badly. Sometimes she worked hard. Sometimes she was idle. Sometimes she got on with her friends. Sometimes she had a row with them. She was just about average, was Gail.

But there was one thing different about her.

She had one funny habit.

Gail kissed frogs.

Well, she tried. It's not all that

easy. It seems easy enough. Frogs sit there very quiet under a stone or a leaf. They don't move. They don't even blink when you look at them. And, their lips stick out a bit, as though they're waiting for someone to give them a big kiss.

But you try and do it.

For one thing. You have to get your face down two inches off the ground. It's very awkward, but that's the way frogs are made.

The trouble is, once you've got down on your knees, and got your face nice and close, what do they do?

They jump. They jump about three feet, not all that far but a long way for a frog. And it doesn't half put you off if you're trying to kiss one.

But Gail kept trying because she'd read in a book somewhere that when a girl kissed a frog, he turned into a prince. A prince with a castle and about two thousand bags of gold and a father who's just about to pop off and leave his kingdom. Then, there's a big wedding, because the prince is grateful and wants to reward the girl

who kissed him, and they all live happily ever after.

And Gail was quite keen on living happily ever after. There were times when she was fed up with life. She lived at home with her mother. Her dad wasn't around, and her mother had to work hard to keep them both. To make a proper living, they took in lodgers. So Gail and her mother lived in the basement and the lodgers lived upstairs. There was a lot of cooking and washing and cleaning. It went on most evenings and every weekend.

Sometimes Gail helped her mother. Sometimes she didn't feel like it. So her mother would just shrug her shoulders and go on working. Then Gail would feel awful and go and help her.

So, every now and then Gail wished that just for once they could have a house all to themselves and enough money not to have to fry bacon and sausage, and wash up, and take loads of dirty washing down to the launder-ette for other people.

Sometimes, when she was fed up, Gail would go out in the garden at the back. It was a sort of garden. Every now and then her mum would go berserk with spades and forks and rakes. Then she'd give up and the grass would grow back, the weeds would sprout and the place would look like Tarzan's back yard again.

Chapter Two

One day, Gail had a row with her
mother. She went out into the garden
for a sulk. There'd been a shower and
the sun had just come out again.
Everything was damp and steamy. As
Gail got to the bottom of the garden
and looked round for something to
kick, she suddenly had the feeling that
someone was watching her. She
looked around — there was no one
there. But Gail knew she was being
watched.

8

Then she saw it. Sitting under a dock leaf, big beady eyes staring, breathing in and out, was the biggest, fattest, grottiest-looking frog. For a moment or two they looked at each other, then the frog spoke.

"Sweet lady. Please have pity on me."

"You what?" said Gail. She didn't mean to be rude. Her mother was

always trying to get her to say "Beg pardon". But it just came out.

"Have pity on a poor creature in distress," said the frog.

Gail crouched down and very carefully put her face a few inches from the frog's. But it didn't move. Instead it spoke again.   .

"My story," said the frog, "is a long and sad one . . ."

But Gail couldn't wait. She knew what she had to do. She squeezed up her mouth and gave the frog a great big kiss right in the middle of his sentence.

There was a sudden noise like the sound of a blown-up paper bag bursting. Then Gail found herself staring

not at the frog any more, but at a pair
of highly polished leather boots.

Standing in front of her was a tall,
handsome man, with wavy blonde
hair and sky blue eyes, dressed in the
most stunning red and gold uniform.

"Oh great," breathed Gail. "A real
prince. Smashing."

She spread out her arms, went down on one knee and said, "Your humble servant, your Highness."

The prince looked down at her, raised his eyebrows and said, "Oh, blow."

"You wha — I mean, I beg your pardon, your gracious . . ."

"I mean," said the Prince, "you're a bit younger than I expected . . ."

"I'm nearly eleven," retorted Gail, a little more sharply than she meant to. "I'm starting at Hob Lane Comprehensive this autumn."

"Comprehensive?"

The prince looked baffled. Gail didn't try to explain. She guessed he'd never been to a comprehensive school anyway. She was a bit put out, now.

"What's wrong with me? I kissed you, didn't I? I broke the spell. What more did you want?"

The Prince drew himself up a little further.

"There is no need to be impertinent. I am, of course, grateful for your help. But according to the rules I am supposed to marry you. And to be quite frank, you are under age."

"Gail!" Mum was calling from the basement window. "Will you come in? It's going to start raining any minute."

"Won't be a minute, Mum," Gail shouted back. She was thinking fast. This wasn't turning out as she expected. It'd be another five years at least before she could marry the Prince. And how was she going to keep him hanging about till then? She played for time.

"Your Highness. My name is Gail." She waved a hand. "This is our humble abode. Would you care to partake of . . ." She tried to think what they were having for supper and what the posh name for it was. Fish-burgers — oh no.

"You Gail!" Gail nearly jumped out of her skin. Her mother was standing right by her. For a moment Gail thought the Prince was going to be invisible. But no such luck.

"Who's this? And what's he doing in fancy dress? Is he looking for a room? The top one's empty."

At the sound of her voice, the Prince turned round and looked straight at Gail's mother. She blushed and started patting her hair.

16

Oh no, thought Gail, this is getting complicated.

"Er, Prince — I'm afraid I don't know your name. This is my mother."

"Prince Rupert," answered the man. "But, surely not your mother. Perhaps your sister."

Oh, he's one of those, thought Gail. She looked at her mother again, who was going all soppy.

"I'm Jackie, short for Jacqueline," said Mum, her voice going squeaky with embarrassment. "Would you like to come in for a cup of tea?" Mum pulled herself together and started taking charge. They walked towards the back door and Gail trailed along behind. This was not turning out right at all.

Chapter Three

Things got worse. Prince Rupert had a very hearty appetite. He ate six fish-burgers (there were only eight in the packet), and drank seven cups of tea. There was hardly anything left for Gail and her mum, but her mum didn't seem to notice.

Prince Rupert chatted on about life at court, how big the castle was, how many servants, how his father was just about to retire. He explained how happy he'd been until a wicked witch had taken a dislike to the family and put a spell on him. And ever since he'd been living as a frog in this damp hole in the ground.

Huh, thought Gail, this basement isn't much better. The point was how soon could they move into the castle? That's what she wanted to know. But every time she wanted to ask an important question like that, her mum said, "Please don't interrupt, Gail. You were saying, Prince Rupert?"

And Prince Rupert seemed to have forgotten completely which fair maiden had rescued him.

In fact, thought Gail, she was beginning to go off Prince Rupert.

Suddenly she knew what was going to happen. Mum was going to marry Prince Rupert, and she was going to be a prince's step-daughter. That wasn't so good. Gail knew what happened to step-daughters in fairy tales. It was about time she sorted things out.

"I say," she burst out. 'I say' is the posh way you interrupt people. "I say."

Mum and Prince Rupert both stopped talking and looked at her.

"Where is this castle of yours?"

"Why, just a half mile away," answered Prince Rupert.

"Well, there's no castle for miles round here," declared Gail.

"Don't be so rude, Gail," said her mother. But Prince Rupert looked baffled.

"Perhaps," he said loftily, "the wicked witch has enchanted the castle away."

Just my luck, thought Gail. But she wasn't giving up yet. "Where is your father's kingdom, then?"

"Why, all around as far as a man can ride in seven days and seven nights."

"You're joking. This is Westchester," retorted Gail, "and we ought to know. We've lived here all our lives."

Prince Rupert went red in the face.

"How dare you contradict me?" He stood up. "I shall not stay here a moment longer, in this hovel. I shall return to the castle immediately."

Mum jumped up and grabbed the Prince by the arm.

"Now, please, your Highness, do calm down. I'm sure no offence was meant. Please stay the night. I have a room empty."

"There's only the box room," said Gail.

"No there's not," snapped her mother. "The others can all move up one and he can have the best room."

Prince Rupert sat down. "Very well. I will stay the night. And out of gratitude, I shall forget your daughter's impertinence."

Gail was ready to explode. But her mother had already gone to sort things out. The lodgers didn't like it, but before they knew it, they were all shifted up one room and Prince Rupert was fixed up in the best room.

Mum even found an old pair of pyjamas for him.

So Prince Rupert stayed the night, and the next night and the next. He stayed in bed until the afternoon most days and then he would get up for supper, eat a lot, drink some wine or a

bottle of beer, talk a lot about life at court and go to bed again. The lodgers thought it was a bit of a giggle at first, but in the end they got fed up with hearing his stories and went off down the pub.

They got even more fed up because Mum was so busy seeing to Prince Rupert, that she didn't bother about cooking their meals properly or clean-

ing the house — apart from the best room. After a while the other lodgers moved out. They'd had enough of hearing Prince Rupert telling them, "So, I said to the Grand Duke . . ."

But things got worse. Mum was so busy looking after Prince Rupert, laundering and ironing his uniform every day, polishing his boots and serving breakfast and lunch in bed, that she was later and later for work until she got the sack. But she didn't seem to notice.

The rest of the house got emptier and dustier. The weeds and grass in the garden grew like triffids. Prince Rupert lay in bed and called for his breakfast and his supper and his polished boots, and Mum ran to and fro whenever he called.

She began to look so pale and thin that Gail stopped feeling furious with her and began to feel worried. After a few weeks, Mum suddenly got 'flu and had to stay in bed. She didn't really want to, but Gail made her.

Gail stopped off school to look after things. But after two days of Prince

Rupert, and his 'Bring me this, bring me that', she'd had enough. That evening, when Mum was tucked up in bed and Prince Rupert was sitting noshing fried chicken in the best room Gail 'phoned Aunt Mandy. Aunt Mandy was tall and slim like Mum, but just a bit different in her ways. She drove a van for the local council and when she cornered, the old folk would say 'Here comes meals on two wheels'.

Chapter Four

Aunt Mandy arrived early next day and went through the house like a dose of salts. She marched into the best room. Gail closed her ears but she could still hear the banging and shouting. Then Aunt Mandy came out with that lovely red uniform under her arm.

"Right, Gail, stuff that lot in the boiler will you."

Suddenly Prince Rupert appeared

in the doorway, in his underpants. He looked truly ridiculous.

"Where is my uniform, woman?" he demanded.

"Just going up in smoke, your worship", answered Aunt Mandy. "Here." From out of her bag she pulled a pair of jeans and an old shirt. "Now get these on and get out in that garden and start cutting that grass."

Prince Rupert went the colour of his trousers.

"How dare you, you impudent witch."

Aunt Mandy took two steps towards him.

"Do you think I'm a witch?" she said, grinning a wicked grin.

Prince Rupert's face turned the colour of his underpants. Without another word he took the shirt and jeans. He marched off to his room.

"I shall certainly not cut the grass. Get a gardener," he said.

Aunt Mandy put her hands on her hips. "No grass, no breakfast, mate," she said.

Prince Rupert stuck it out until supper time. But next day when Gail came home from school, the garden

was cleared, all the weeds were pulled up. It hadn't looked so good for years. Inside the kitchen Aunt Mandy and Prince Rupert were having a cup of tea. He had a bandage on his hand. Gail felt quite sorry for him.

"Oh, did you cut your hand on the shears?" she asked.

"No, love, he burnt it making a cup of tea. But he's shaping," said Aunt Mandy.

So, it all turned out not too badly after all. Mum got better. She got her job back. And Prince Rupert got a part-time job at the Bingo Club. When he called out, "All the sevens" in that posh voice of his, the old ladies loved it.

They didn't earn much, but it was enough for the three of them. And they didn't bother with lodgers any more. So Gail was able to live in the whole house after all. She got to quite like Rupert in the end — though not as much as her mum did.

So they all lived happily ever after.

Then one day, after it had been raining, Gail was out in the garden pulling up the odd weed in the flower bed. As she bent down, she had the feeling someone was watching her.

And there under the azalea sat the biggest, fattest, grottiest-looking frog you ever saw, gazing at her with his great, beady eyes.

Then he spoke.

"Sweet lady. Have pity on me."

Gail looked him straight in the eye.
"Listen, buster. You have one
minute to get out of here."